The EYE Book

by Theo. LeSieg

Illustrated by

Roy McKie

COLLINS

Trademark of Random House, Inc., William Collins Sons & Co. Ltd., Authorised User

1 2 3 4 5 6 7 8 9 10

ISBN 0 00 171288 8 (paperback)

ISBN 0 00 171201 2 (hardback)

Copyright © 1968 by Random House, Inc.
A Bright and Early Book for Beginning Beginners
Published by arrangement with Random House, Inc.,
New York, New York
First Published in Great Britain 1969
Printed & bound in Hong Kong

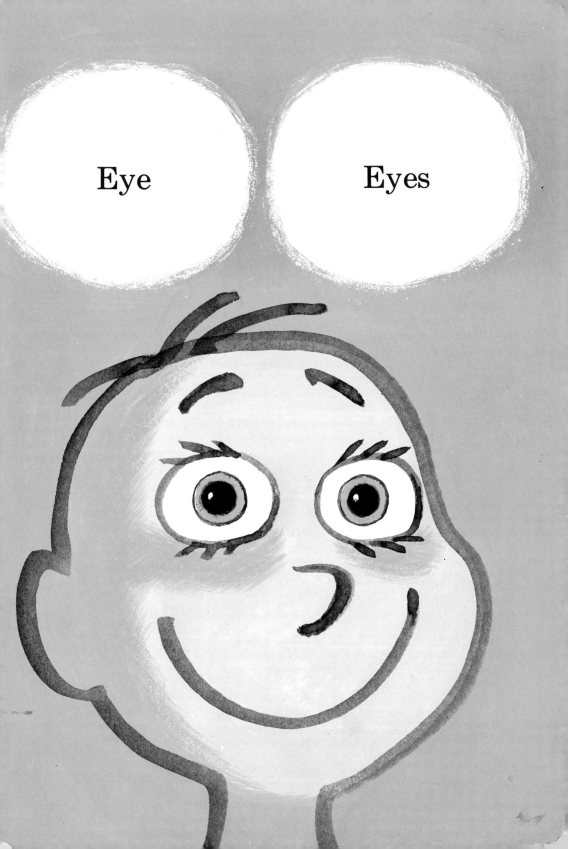

My eyes
My eyes

His eyes
His eyes

Wink eye
Wink eye

Pink eye  Pink eye

My eyes see.

His eyes see.

I see him.

And he sees me.

Our eyes see blue.

Our eyes see red.

They see a bird.

They see a bed.

They see the sun.

They see the moon.

They see a fork

a knife

a spoon.

They see a girl.

They see a man . . .

a boy

a horse

an old tin can.

They look down holes.

They look up poles.

Our eyes see trees.

They look at clocks.

They look at bees.

They look at socks.

Our eyes see flies.

Our eyes see ants.

Sometimes they see
pink underpants.

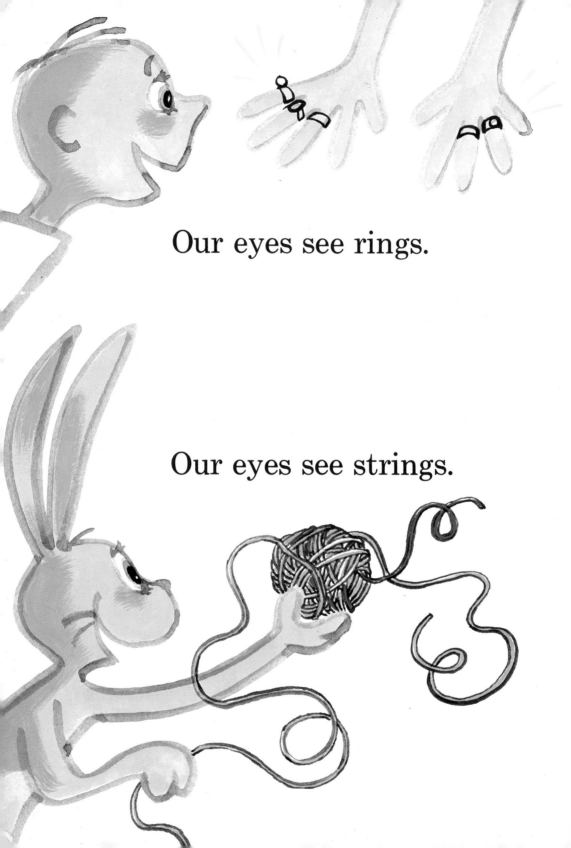

Our eyes see rings.

Our eyes see strings.

They see
so many, many things!

So many things!

Like rain

and pie . . .

and dogs

and aeroplanes
in the sky!

And so we say,
"Hooray for eyes!
Hooray, hooray, hooray . . .

. . . for eyes!"